Kirsten Peters

The
Gigantic
Turnip

For Owen — N. S.

Barefoot Books
37 West 17th Street
4th Floor East
New York, New York 10011

This book is printed on 100% acid-free paper

Graphic design by Tom Grzelinski, England
Color separation by Grafiscan, Italy
Printed and bound in Singapore by Tien Wah Press (Pte) Ltd

1 3 5 7 9 8 6 4 2

Cataloging data prepared for the hardback edition (1999):

U.S. Cataloging-in-Publication Data / Library of Congress Standards

Tolstoy, Aleksei.
    The gigantic turnip / Aleksei Tolstoy and Niamh Sharkey.
[40] p. : col. ill. ; 28 cm.
Summary: A hilarious retelling of the famous Russian folktale
of the turnip that grows and grows and grows. Simple vocabulary,
lots of repetition, and quirky illustrations add to its overall appeal.
ISBN: 1-902283-12-0 ISBN: 1-84148-157-2 (pbk.)
    1. Folklore -- Russia. I. Sharkey, Niamh. II. Title.
398.2/ 0947 --dc21   1999   AC   CIP

The Gigantic Turnip

Aleksei Tolstoy & Niamh Sharkey

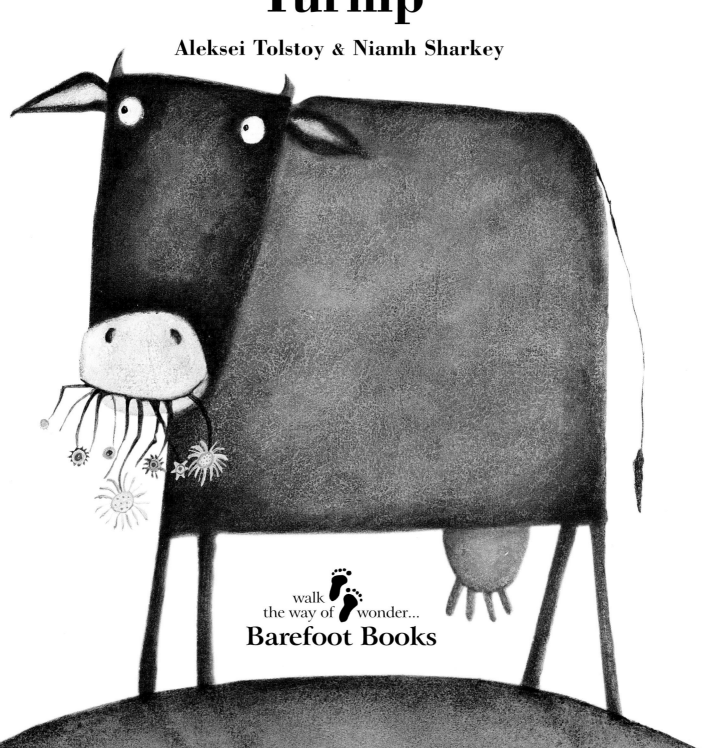

walk
the way of wonder...
Barefoot Books

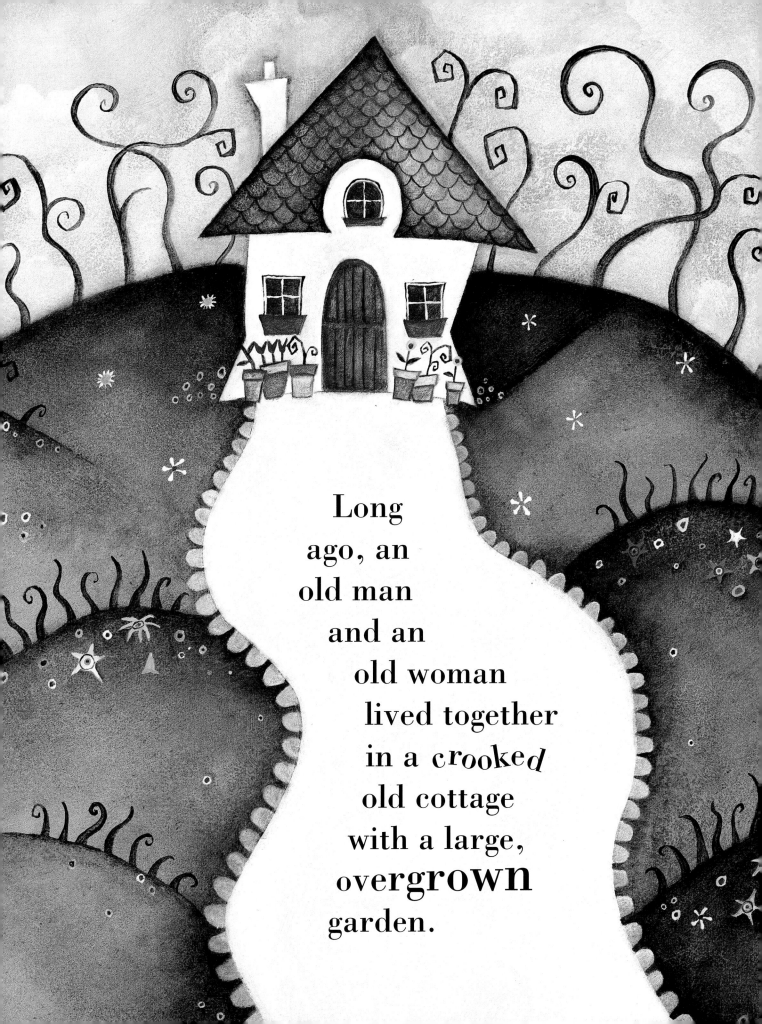

Long
ago, an
old man
and an
old woman
lived together
in a crooked
old cottage
with a large,
overgrown
garden.

The old man
and the old
woman

kept six yellow canaries,

five white geese,

On a fine March morning, the old woman sat up in bed, sniffed the sweet spring air and said, "It's time for us to sow the vegetables!" So the old man and the old woman went out into the garden.

They sowed peas and carrots
and potatoes and beans. Last of
all, they sowed
turnips.

That night, rain fell — pitter, patter! — on the garden of the crooked old cottage. The old man and the old woman smiled as they slept.

The rain would help the seeds swell and produce fine juicy vegetables.

Spring passed and the summer sun ripened the vegetables. The old man and the old woman harvested their carrots and potatoes and peas and beans and turnips. At the end of the row, there was just one turnip left. It looked very big.
In fact, it looked

gigantic.

On a fine
September
morning, the
old man sat up
in bed, sniffed
the cool fall air
and said,
"It's time for us to
pull up that turnip."

And out he went.

The old man pulled and heaved and tugged and yanked, but the turnip would not move.

The old man went to find the old woman.

The old woman wrapped
her arms round the old
man's waist. Both of
them pulled and heaved
and tugged and yanked,
but still the turnip would
not move.

So the old woman went to
fetch the big brown cow.

The old man, the old woman and the
big brown cow pulled and heaved
and tugged and yanked, but still the
turnip would not move.

So the old man mopped his brow and
went to fetch the two pot-bellied pigs.

The old man, the old woman, the big brown cow and the two pot-bellied pigs pulled and heaved and tugged and yanked. Still the turnip would not move.

So the old woman rolled up her sleeves and went to fetch the three black cats.

The old man, the old woman, the big brown cow, the two pot-bellied pigs and the three black cats pulled and heaved and tugged and yanked. Still the turnip would not move.

So one of the cats twitched her tail and went to fetch the four speckled hens.

The old man, the old
woman, the big brown
cow, the two pot-bellied
pigs, the three black cats
and the four speckled
hens pulled and heaved
and tugged and yanked.
Still the turnip would
not move.

So one of the hens shook
her feathers and went to
fetch the five white geese.

The old man, the old woman, the big brown cow, the two pot-bellied pigs, the three black cats, the four speckled hens and the five white geese pulled and heaved and tugged and yanked. Still the turnip would not move.

So one of the geese
craned her neck and
went to fetch the
six yellow canaries.

The old man, the old woman, the big brown cow, the two pot-bellied pigs, the three black cats, the four speckled hens,

the five white geese and the
six yellow canaries pulled
and heaved and tugged
and yanked.

Still the turnip would not move.

The old man scratched his head.

The animals and birds lay
on the ground gasping.

The old woman had an idea.

The old woman went
into the kitchen and
put a piece of cheese
by the mousehole.
Soon a hungry little
mouse popped its
head out of the hole.
The old woman
caught the mouse and
carried it outside.

The old man, the old
woman, the big brown
cow, the two pot-bellied
pigs, the three black cats,
the four speckled hens,

the five white geese, the
six yellow canaries and the
hungry little mouse pulled
and heaved and tugged
and yanked.

Pop!

The gigantic turnip came flying out of the ground and everyone fell over. The canaries fell on the mouse, the geese fell on the canaries, the hens fell on the geese, the cats fell on the hens, the pigs fell on the cats, the cow fell on the pigs, the old woman fell on the cow and the old man fell on the old woman.

All of them lay on the ground and laughed.

That night the old man and
the old woman made a huge
bowl of turnip stew.
Everyone ate as much as
they could. And do you know
what? The hungry little
mouse ate the most of all.